A Parents Magazine
READ ALOUD AND EASY READING PROGRAM® Original.

Distributed in Canada by Clarke, Irwin & Co., Ltd.
Toronto, Canada

The LAKE MESS MONSTER

Beverly Komoda

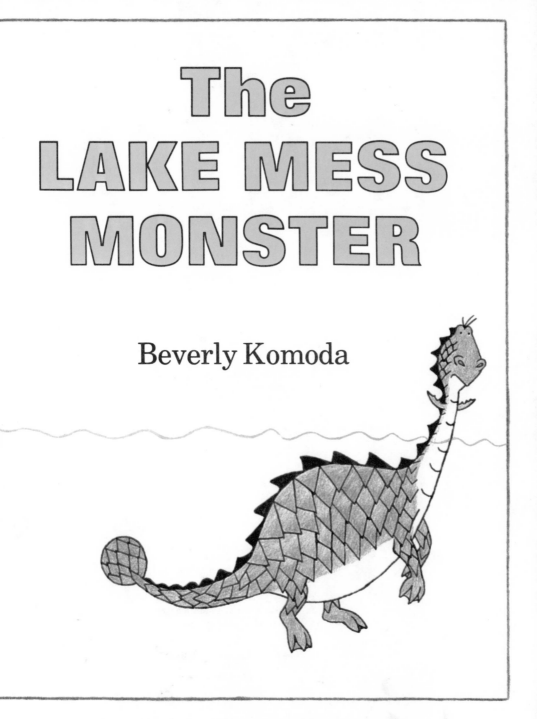

PARENTS MAGAZINE PRESS • NEW YORK

Copyright © 1980 by Beverly Komoda.
All rights reserved.
Printed in the United States of America.
10 9 8 7 6 5 4 3 2

Library of Congress Cataloging in Publication Data
Komoda, Beverly. The Lake Mess monster.
SUMMARY: When a belligerent monster appears in
Lake Mess, the people who have always enjoyed the lake
must find a way for them all to use the lake amicably.
[1. Monsters—Fiction]   I. Title.
PZ7.K8348Lak   [E]   80–17569
ISBN 0–8193–1033–6   ISBN 0–8193–1034–4 (lib. bdg.)

For Mary and Robert Higashida

Where's the best place to
swim, fish, or boat?
"Lake Mess!" the old-timers said.
Someone from Harry Mess's family

had always lived on the lake shore.
That's how the lake got its name.
One summer day, people were enjoying
the lake as they always did.

Harry Mess and his sister, Sandy,
were hunting minnows when...

the fish started acting up!

Harry pointed out to the middle
of the lake and shouted, "LOOK!"
A scaly head on a long neck
rose out of the water.

Swimmers left the water fast!
The boats tried to get in to shore.
Most of them made it.

"We've got ourselves a monster,"
said Grandpa Mess.

"Maybe he's a friendly one, Grandpa,"
said Sandy.

The monster went for the boats
still out on the lake.
He tipped them over and

dunked every person in sight.
Binny Whipple howled and
called him names when he dunked her.

The monster dunked Binny nine times more.
"He's a MEAN one!" said Harry.

Harry and Sandy's pa, Dandy, got up
a group to go catch the beast.

But no sooner did their boat
get into the water than that monster
whacked them right back out again
with his tail.

Harry and Sandy jumped up and down.
"That monster thinks this lake is his!"
shouted Sandy.

"He'll hog the lake all summer!"
yelled Harry.

"Where did he come from?" asked Dandy.

"Must have been the underground stream into the lake, Pa," said Harry.
"He could have swum through —
from who knows where!"

The group got a bigger boat...
and a fishing net. They tried again.

This time they got close enough
to throw the net.

It didn't work.

The monster looked as if
he were laughing.
He whacked the big boat
out of the water, too!

"How do we get rid of the pesky critter?" asked Dandy.

"Fast!" said Binny Whipple.
"I'm going with you next time!"

"Hook him like a fish!" said Purty, Harry and Sandy's ma.

The group and Binny got an even bigger boat.

Everybody tried, but no hook and line
was big enough.

The monster chewed off all the lines
and still looked as if he were laughing.

Then he shoved the big boat
right back to the shore!

"I'm going to get you!" screeched Binny.
"No one dunks Binny Whipple."

"Hold on there, Binny," said Dandy.

"We could leave him be," said Sandy.
"I think he could be nice."

"So do I," said Grandpa Mess.
"We'll make do with what we have!"

"We've got ourselves a monster!"
said Harry. "Nobody else
in the county can say that!"

The monster spurted water at them like a fire hose.

"He's mean!" squawked Binny.

"He's unhappy," said Sandy.

"Then let's make the critter happy,"
said Harry.

"Yuk!" said Binny.
And she shook her fist at the beast.

The monster moved in close to shore.
Everybody ran.

He took aim and spurted water,
hitting Binny dead center!

Then the monster dove to the lake bottom
and came up with a tin can.
He whacked it at the people with his tail.
He dove again and whacked
a pair of sunglasses at them.

Faster and faster he dove and whacked.
Everybody ducked and danced
as things flew through the air.
"Why is he unhappy?" shouted Purty.
"He's got fish to eat."

"Maybe he's lonely," said Sandy.
"He wants to play,
but everybody gets mad at him."

The monster slapped water at them.

"Where can we get a friend
for a monster?" said Dandy.
He leaped aside as water splashed down.

"Wait a minute!" Harry yelled.

He ran up the beach and came back
carrying a plastic float toy.
It was fat and pink with yellow spots
and a big silly smile.
"How about this?" he asked.

"I wish we had a real live friend
for the critter!" said Sandy.

"But we don't," said Grandpa.
"We have to make do. Try it, Harry.
Quick, float it out on the lake!"
Harry pushed the toy away from shore.

SPLASH!
The monster went for the toy right away.
He bumped it. He dunked it.
It popped right back up,
wearing that big silly smile.
The monster cuddled up to it.
"He likes it!" Harry shouted.

"Everybody run and find more
float toys!" yelled Dandy.
They did, and pushed the toys
out on the lake.

"That monster is happy!" said Harry.

The monster swam in circles,
showing off for his new friends.
The toys bobbed around him in the
water, smiling their painted smiles.

Harry laughed. "People don't like
his way of playing,
but his new friends do!"

Well, the people got used to the monster...

and he got used to the people.

The only thing is,
they had to float out
new toys every few days
when the old ones wore out.

"No problem," said Dandy.

"None at all!" said Harry.
"We've got ourselves a monster."

ABOUT THE AUTHOR/ARTIST

BEVERLY KOMODA has illustrated several picture books and is the author as well of *Simon's Soup*. She says that ideas for stories come to her while she is doing routine or boring things—such as riding the New York subways or doing the laundry.

The Lake Mess Monster is based on memories of Whipple's Dam, a lake where she and her friends used to go swimming when she was growing up. "The characters in this story—including the monster— are bits and pieces of people I have known," she says.

Beverly Komoda lives in East Windsor, New Jersey, with her husband, who is an art director and illustrator, and their three sons, who are all artists too. "We use a lot of paper, pencils, and ink at our house!" she explains.